M000014899

ONE WRIGHT STAND

ONE WRIGHT STAND

K.A. LINDE

ALSO BY K. A. LINDE

WRIGHTS

The Wright Brother | The Wright Boss

The Wright Mistake | The Wright Secret

The Wright Love | The Wright One

A Wright Christmas | One Wright Stand

Wright with Benefits | Serves Me Wright

CRUEL

One Cruel Night | Cruel Money

Cruel Fortune | Cruel Legacy

Cruel Promise | Cruel Truth

Cruel Desire | Cruel Marriage

RECORD SERIES

Off the Record | On the Record | For the Record

Struck from the Record | Broken Record

AVOIDING SERIES

Avoiding Commitment | Avoiding Responsibility

Avoiding Temptation | Avoiding Extras | Avoiding Boxset

DIAMOND GIRLS SERIES

Rock Hard | A Girl's Best Friend

In the Rough | Shine Bright

Under Pressure

TAKE ME DUET

Take Me for Granted | Take Me with You

STAND ALONE

Following Me

Hold the Forevers

FANTASY ROMANCE

BLOOD TYPE SERIES

Blood Type | Blood Match | Blood Cure

ASCENSION SERIES

The Affiliate | The Bound | The Consort

The Society | The Domina

ROYAL HOUSES

House of Dragons | House of Shadows

One Wright Stand
Copyright © 2021 by K.A. Linde
All rights reserved.

Visit my website at
www.kalinde.com

Cover Designer: Okay Creations.,
www.okaycreations.com
Photography: Wander Aguiar Photography,
www.wanderaguiar.com
Editor: Unforeseen Editing,
www.unforeseenediting.com

No part of this book may be reproduced or transmitted in any
form or by any means, electronic or mechanical, including
photocopying, recording, or by any information storage and
retrieval system without the written permission of the author,
except for the use of brief quotations in a book review.

This book is a work of fiction. Names, characters, places, and
incidents either are products of the author's imagination or are
used fictitiously. Any resemblance to actual persons, living or
dead, events, or locales is entirely coincidental.

ISBN-13: 978-1948427456

1

ANNIE

*O*n a scale from one to boring, I'd hit my max three days ago.

Logically, I'd known that medical school was going to be a challenge, but the past week of orientation had been so mind-numbingly dull that I could hardly stand it. Eight hours a day, stuck in an auditorium, listening to introductory information, had meant only one thing when it was over—drinks.

"Whoa! Annie, slow down," Cézanne said. She plucked the beer out of my hand and set it back down on the bar.

"Oh, come on. You were in the same meetings with me all week. You must have been dying for this happy hour."

Cézanne shook her head, swinging her signature

box braids. "Some of us actually enjoy school. That's why we're here."

I grinned at my friend, all tall, slinky grace with dark brown skin that practically glowed in the incandescent overhead lighting. We'd had several chemistry and anatomy classes together in undergrad at Texas Tech. While I'd spent the last year working as a receptionist at a dental office, Cézanne had gotten a Masters in statistics. They'd wanted to fast-track her into the PhD program, but medicine was her true passion.

"I'm not here to enjoy school. I'm here to become a doctor."

After the last couple of years, that was all I really wanted. Losing two people close to me had made it a necessity. I couldn't stand on the sidelines as someone died and not come out of it changed. Next time, I wanted to be the person who could do something about it.

"Anyway, let's talk about more important things," I said, snatching back my beer and taking another swig. "Like who the hottest guys in our class are."

Cézanne eyes drifted to the ceiling. "Lord, help me."

"You're absolutely right. I should be looking at second years and up." I grinned at her and tugged my long red hair out of its ponytail. The strands fell in a wave just past the shoulders of my black V-neck T-shirt. I messed with my hair in the camera on my phone, checking my pink lipstick and how clear my freckles were through the sheer layer of my pale foundation. Good enough.

"Can't you just pick one man and settle down?" Cézanne complained.

"I could, but what would be the fun in that?" I eyed my friend. "It's not like you're settled."

Cézanne shrugged. "I haven't found the right guy."

"Sure," I drawled sarcastically. "Me either."

Cézanne snorted.

My eyes roamed Walkers, a coffee shop by day and grad school bar by night. The room was already packed for the afternoon happy hour. Honestly, it was a little embarrassing that so many of my class-mates were still wearing their white coat *inside*. We'd gotten it during orientation, marking us as official medical students in training. I'd taken the requisite pictures to post all over social media, but I hadn't exactly planned to wear it out. They must have thought it was going to help them get laid, or they thought very highly of themselves.

My gaze shifted to the entrance. "Do you see what I see?"

Cézanne nodded next to me. "Uh...yeah. Okay, you win. I don't know what year he is, but he is *right* up your alley."

I laughed but didn't disagree. Mr. Tall, Dark, and Handsome was definitely my type. At least, if I had a type, he'd be it. His khakis were pressed, and the sleeves of his light-blue button-up shirt were rolled to his elbows. He had on polished leather dress shoes. Not cheap loafers or boat shoes and definitely not cowboy boots, which were always hit or miss in middle-of-nowhere West Texas. He was couth with his gelled dark brown hair and chiseled jaw. He looked more like he'd walked out of a *GQ* spread than into a dusty bar in Lubbock, Texas.

So what the hell was he doing here?

Despite the sheer number of people in the room at five o'clock in the afternoon, he navigated it with ease. Just as he approached, I swiveled around to face the bar. Cézanne shot me a questioning look and huffed when I winked at her.

"Excuse me," he said, his voice deep.

I shifted to the side, giving him enough room to wedge himself in front of the bar. "Sorry about that."

He glanced in my direction. "Why is this place so packed?"

I met his gaze, a shiver running down my spine. Anything I'd thought about him being my type before was completely blown out of the water when I got a good look at that face. Strong lines and high cheekbones and full, almost-pouty lips with eyes the deepest, darkest brown that bored into my very soul.

"I guess no one told you about the med school happy hour?"

"I unfortunately didn't get that memo."

"Well, your loss is my gain," I said with a laugh.

He arched an eyebrow and quirked his lips. "Is that so?"

"Well, I sure think so." I stuck my hand out. "I'm Annie."

He shook my hand with the strength and power of a man who knew what he wanted. "Jordan."

"Nice to meet you. I'm guessing you're not a med student."

"That I'm not." His eyes drifted around the room. "Is it normal for you to be wearing the jacket in public?"

I chuckled. "No. It's kind of ridiculous, right?"

"Definitely surprising. I was told this was a good place to get coffee."

"It is during the day, but after five, it's primarily a bar." I gestured to the rows of booths still cluttered with laptops and paperwork. "It's why all the grad students come here."

"They still serve coffee after five? It would suck to have driven all the way out here for nothing."

I shot him a dimpled grin. "Don't worry about it. I know the bartender. He's a morning barista. I'm sure he'll hook you up." With a heft upward, I leaned over the bar, revealing my ass in all its glory in my favorite frayed jean shorts. "Ken!"

I could feel Jordan's eyes on me as I flagged down my favorite bartender. Ken waved me off, letting me know he'd seen me, and I hopped back down. My foot caught the bottom of the railing wrong, and my ankle rolled.

"Oof," I gasped, sliding sideways into the stranger. "Sorry."

His strong arms held me in place, righting me back onto my feet. "Are you all right?"

"Yeah. I always forget about this." I gently toed the bottom step.

I reluctantly backed out of his arms as Ken appeared before us.

"Hey, Barbie. What can I get you?" Ken asked.

I rolled my eyes. "Coffee for my friend here."

Jordan leaned in. "I'll take a latte with a double shot of espresso."

"You got it."

"Barbie?" Jordan asked with an arched eyebrow as Ken went for his order.

"Ugh. It's a stupid nickname that I got in high school. Ken and Barbie." I shrugged. "It stuck."

"I would have thought they'd bestow that title on a blonde." He fingered a loose strand of my dark auburn hair.

"Trust me, it was actually better than being a redhead named Annie."

He chuckled. "I could see that."

"Here you go, bro," Ken said, sliding Jordan's drink across the bar.

Jordan passed him cash. "Keep the change."

"You got it." Ken nodded and then disappeared back into the crowd desperate for more libations.

"Hey," I said, putting a hand on his forearm. Might as well go for it. He was hot. What did I have to lose? "Maybe you could stay and party with us tonight."

He shot me another one of those heart-melting smiles. "I wish I could. But unfortunately, I have family obligations."

"Bummer," I said, sticking my bottom lip out slightly.

"It is."

"I think we'll be here again tomorrow night," I suggested

"I'll see if I can get away. Thanks for the coffee and conversation, Annie."

"Yeah," I said with a smile. "It was my pleasure."

Then I watched him walk away. My heart still beat a frantic note in my chest, telling me to run after him. He was too damn gorgeous. I wanted to get to know him. I wanted to know what someone dressed like that was doing in Lubbock. I didn't know why, but I couldn't shake the feeling that I was making a huge mistake.

"Oh, girl, did you get his number?" Cézanne asked, reappearing at precisely the right time.

"Fuck," I hissed. "I never asked for it."

"What were you thinking?"

I didn't know. I hadn't been thinking in his presence. I'd just...existed in a bubble with him. And I'd wanted it to last longer.

I might never see him again. And I'd totally blown my chance.

2

ANNIE

*C*ézanne had kept me out *way* too late. Or maybe I'd kept her out too late. Either way, the next morning, I was feeling the side effects.

I popped two Tylenol and downed a bottle of Gatorade as I leaned back against the refrigerator. My head was spinning. I wasn't sure I was even hungover. I might still be drunk. How many shots had I taken? The number eluded me. As did how I'd gotten home.

"Annie, is that you?" my roommate, Jennifer, asked as she entered the kitchen.

"Yep," I muttered.

Jennifer and I were as opposite as opposite could be. We'd gone to high school together, but while I'd been the head cheerleader, she'd been the quiet, shy yearbook nerd. I'd worn designer clothes while she'd been in hand-me-downs. I cringed now when I thought about how judgmental I'd been then. Because Jennifer Gibson was quite possibly the nicest, most unassuming person I'd ever met.

She never judged me for dicking around or drinking until I was still drunk the next morning. Somehow, she found the whole thing endearing even. And I was grateful that we'd moved in together after reconnecting through our best friend, Sutton Wright.

"Wow. You look..."

"Still drunk," I offered.

"A bit, yeah," Jennifer confessed with a wince. "You're still planning to go to the Wright pool party, right?"

"Fuck."

"Welp," Jennifer said with a laugh, "you could stay here and sleep it off."

I massaged my temples. "No, it's Landon's big day. He's going back to the PGA after this weekend. I can't miss it."

The Wrights were as close as Lubbock got to royalty. They owned Wright Construction, a Fortune 500 company and the largest construction company in the United States. Jensen, Austin, Landon,

Morgan, and Sutton were likely the most well-known people in this city. I'd grown up with Sutton, admiring her older brothers and sister, watching Jensen all but raise them after their parents passed, and seeing them one by one make a name for themselves on their own all while finding their one true pairing.

Even Sutton had, and along came baby Jason... until tragedy hit. I closed my eyes against the reminder. I'd been there that day. I'd been standing next to her husband Maverick when he collapsed.

"Hey, are you okay?" Jennifer asked.

"Fine," I said at once, pushing those thoughts out of my head. "Just a headache."

This was why I'd wanted to become a doctor. I could have fixed it. I could have helped.

"Okay," Jennifer said. "I can drive if you want to get dressed."

"Sounds good. The Tylenol will kick in soon."

I worked for a smile as I passed my roommate. It came out as more of a grimace.

I'd definitely forgotten about Landon's party last night when I got hammered, and I was paying for it today.

My phone buzzed where I'd thankfully plugged it in last night. Cézanne had sent a handful of messages, and I skimmed them as I went in search of a bathing suit.

You still drunk, child?

I laughed and rolled my eyes. She was only six months older than me, but she'd been calling me child for as long as I'd known her.

A bit. I forgot I had a pool party this morning. Sunshine and loud music...just what I need.

You poor thing. Suffering at a pool party. <insert eye roll>

Oh, Cézanne. I tugged on a forest-green bikini with pink and white flowers on it, then my favorite black cover-up, which showed off my milky-white legs, a floppy hat to protect me against the beat of the sun, and oversize glasses...so hopefully not everyone would notice I was a hot mess.

Twenty minutes later, after Jennifer had packed the essentials and made me eat something, we were in her tiny Honda Civic. The AC had sputtering fits and only worked on days that Jennifer cussed it out. Sweet little thing. It made my heart soar to hear her get so mad at the vehicle.

"I swear...this fucking thing," she spat, hitting the console as she headed toward Landon's house. "You piece of shit."

The car must have heard her because cool air

finally came out of the vents, and I leaned my drunk head against them, saying a prayer to whoever was listening.

"We could have taken my car."

Jennifer side-eyed me. "Bertha works just fine."

"Bertha needs new AC."

"Don't even with me right now, Annie."

I grinned. I wasn't wrong. But where the money for that was going to come from was up for debate.

We arrived at Landon's house without incident. He lived way on the outskirts of the south side of town, where all the new money was trying to escape the expansion. He'd built the Wright golf course over the last year and had its first tournament this summer. It was a sprawling PGA-approved course, and he lived right on the eighteenth hole with his beautiful girlfriend, Heidi.

Jennifer parked Bertha down the street from the mansion on the only hill in Lubbock, and we hiked up to the front door with our provisions. Jennifer knocked twice and waited, fidgeting with her hands as if she couldn't possibly stay still.

Heidi wrenched the door open. "Hey, girls!"

"Hey, Heidi," I said with a smile. "You look great."

"Thanks."

"Hi," Jennifer said, reaching into her bag and

pulling out her trusty camera. "I thought I could take some pictures."

"Yes! Oh my God, I'd love that." Heidi pulled the door wide and glanced over at her best friend, Emery. "Wouldn't you love that, Em?"

"Hmm?" she asked, pulling herself out of the giant novel she was reading.

"Having your picture taken?"

Emery narrowed her eyes at Heidi. "I hate you."

"Right back at you," she said with a laugh. She turned back to us. "Well, come on in. Jensen and Landon are working on the grill out back. There are drinks in the fridge, if you want anything, and Julia and I put together some finger food in the kitchen. Help yourself."

"Sutton here yet?" I asked.

Heidi shook her head. "I haven't seen her or her little cutie, but I'm sure she'll be here soon."

Heidi winked at us, her blonde ponytail bouncing as she rushed over to Emery and poked her in the side. Emery rolled her eyes and playfully smacked her with the book.

"I think I need a drink," I told Jennifer.

"A drink? Aren't you still drunk?"

"Just one...so I can function."

"You're a mess."

"True story. But after this weekend, it's serious Annie all the time. Medical school is no joke, and I want to get all of my fun out before I spend the next four years studying my ass off."

Jennifer immediately softened. "Of course. You're right. You should have fun. You'll be so busy later."

"You will, too! As soon as you get that pharmacy school application in."

Jennifer's cheeks colored. "Yes...just as soon as I do that."

I ruffled her blonde hair and then grabbed a beer out of the fridge. Jennifer disappeared, clicking away with her Canon Rebel like the professional I *knew* she wanted to be. She always *said* pharmacy school was her dream, but she had major parental pressure. It sure didn't help that her older brother was a genius, but it didn't excuse them not seeing her own passion. The only time she really lit up was when that camera was in front of her face. I sure hoped one day she'd see that, too.

I tipped back the beer, trying to shake off the lingering hangover. I was serious about buckling down once I started school on Monday. Of course, I'd still be around. Jensen and Emery's wedding was coming up, which I had no plans of missing. But the Annie who everyone knew from the last couple years would soon be gone. I couldn't afford to fuck this up. Not when I really, *really* wanted this.

So, I'd have my last week of fun, easygoing, flirtatious Annie. Then it was good-bye freedom and hello medical school.

I downed the rest of the beer and tossed it into the recycling. I grabbed another because why not? Then I stripped out of my cover-up and leaned against the back doorframe as I observed the pool party in full swing.

The rectangular-shaped pool was enormous with a diving board and spa. Already, kids were splashing in the shallow end while guys in board shorts and six-packs tried to coax each other into more outrageous feats off the diving board. Heidi, Emery, and Julia had migrated to beach chairs, where Heidi had lathered up in oil, Emery continued to read her book, and Julia hid her face under a low-hanging baseball cap. As promised, Jensen and Landon were grilling. Jennifer took pictures of the event, careful to keep back from the pool with her precious baby.

And then my eyes snapped to a person who was completely out of place.

"Oh my God," I whispered.

The hot guy from the bar was *here*.

3

ANNIE

I blinked rapidly. I must be hallucinating. What the fuck was Jordan doing at a Wright pool party?

He stood near the grill, observing what was happening but not interfering. He held a beer in his hand and sipped it absentmindedly. And dear fucking God, he was in nothing but short blue swim trunks. The kind reserved for surfers who wanted to show off their tanned, muscular thighs...which he had...and the ripped fucking six-pack, which he also had, and that goddamn V that ended somewhere in his shorts. My mind went fuzzy at the thought of what was underneath that. Because yes, please, and thank you.

I didn't think. I just reacted, striding across the tiled pool walkway, straight to where he stood.

His eyes flickered over to me for a second, and then he did a double take, as if realizing the same thing that I just had.

I ate up the rest of the steps and then stopped directly in front of him.

"Annie?" he said, as if conjuring my name from thin air.

"Family obligations, huh?"

He laughed, and I melted at the sound. "What are you doing here?"

"Me? This is a Wright pool party. Sutton Wright is my best friend. What exactly are *you* doing here?"

He grinned devilishly, and for a second, I imagined all the ways he could use that perfect mouth on my body. He held his hand out. "I believe we should start over."

I slid my hand into his. "Okay?"

"I'm Jordan. Jordan Wright."

My heart stopped beating. "Jordan...Wright," I breathed. "As in...you're the Wright cousin. The one from...Canada?"

"That's me."

"Oh," I squeaked.

He still hadn't released my hand. "It's a pleasure to meet you again, Annie. Though unexpected."

Unexpected was an understatement. Now that I saw it, I couldn't unsee it. Of course, Jordan was a Wright. He had the same characteristic smile and those deep, dark eyes and that style that only money could possibly buy. No *wonder* I'd been immediately into him. I'd had a childhood crush on all three of Sutton's completely unattainable, older brothers. But friendship was more important than anything.

Sutton had one rule to our friendship: her brothers were off-limits.

But she hadn't said *anything* about her cousins.

Well, this had taken a turn in my favor.

Not just because he was a Wright, of course. That was a bonus. I'd been into Jordan the minute I saw him walk into that bar, and I'd kicked myself all night for not getting his number. I had no intention of wasting the opportunity a second time.

"Well, I think the pleasure is all mine," I finally managed to get out.

He smiled at my reaction. An honest smile. He was actually pleased to see me. A thrill shot down my spine.

I slowly extracted my hand from his and brushed a lock of my auburn hair behind my ear. I couldn't keep a smile from my face. What was it about this guy that turned me into a puddle?

"Funny that we keep running into each other. Everyone here tried to reassure me that this isn't a small town."

"Well, I mean...it's not. It's big enough, but it's not as big as...wherever you're from, I'm sure." I tried to recall if Sutton had mentioned where her cousins were from. She hadn't told me they were hot, so I hadn't been paying attention. "Where are you from again?"

"Vancouver. And yeah, Lubbock is tiny in comparison."

"I'm of the opinion that the universe puts people in our path. Doesn't really matter the size of the town."

"I guess I have the universe to thank then."

My heart skipped a beat. Oh, he was good. Charming and confident and so fucking good-looking. I was in trouble...or maybe he was.

Then Sutton stride into the backyard with her two-year-old son, Jason, in tow. I waved at the pair of them. Sutton's eyes found mine, and she returned the gesture.

But despite her quirked lips and wave, she didn't look great. She looked...tired. I felt for my friend.

The last year had been rough. After Maverick had died, I'd watched her go from happy-go-lucky party girl to a shell of her former self.

Everyone had noticed her change at first, of course. But a year later, most people thought she was coming around. That things were A-OK again. Or if not perfect, at least she was moving on.

I wished that I saw the same thing. Instead, I saw my friend barely functioning. That her son was the only thing keeping her afloat. She needed to catch a break soon.

"Is she all right?" Jordan asked with a furrowed brow.

I jolted. "What do you mean?"

"She looks so...well, sad."

My mind froze as I looked up at this man. He didn't even know Sutton, and somehow, he could see what others couldn't? That she was a mess.

"You can tell she's sad?"

"I mean...look at her."

"I know," I whispered softly. "She's been through a lot. She's been my best friend since we were kids, and it's so hard to see her like this. I wish there was more that I could do."

"I get that," he said easily, his eyes sliding to his brother. "I've been protecting my brother my entire life. There are just some things you can't protect people from."

"So true."

Sutton set her stuff aside, put floaties on Jason, and then got into the pool. Emery's sister, Kimber, was there with her kids, and Jason gravitated to the two older girls to play with them. Jennifer left her camera on a lounge chair and walked into the pool to say hi to Sutton. Then they both turned and looked at me at the same time.

I would have been offended if I hadn't seen that *exact* look more times than I could count. Their eyes flitted between me and Jordan, wondering how much of a mess I was getting myself into.

Sutton arched an eyebrow. Her words were clear in my head.

Don't you dare, Annie.

I grinned devilishly back at her. *Oh, I dare, Sut. I definitely dare.*

Sutton rolled her eyes. *You're the worst. You and your games.*

Just one more weekend, I pleaded with my best friend. *Then it's good-bye flirtatious Annie forever.*

She laughed at our silent argument and turned her back on me. She thought that I was trouble. I always had been in the past. There was only one guy

I'd ever been serious about, and otherwise, I just liked to have a lot of fun. I didn't think there was anything wrong with that, but she still worried. She couldn't take another heartbreak.

Not that I had any interest in love or broken hearts or anything. But Jordan Wright was introspective and gorgeous and right fucking here. He'd been put in my path now...*twice*. The universe was practically offering him to me on a silver platter. Wouldn't it be wrong to do nothing?

4

ANNIE

*M*y green eyes were wide with innocence when I turned back to Jordan. I needed to shift the conversation away from Sutton and back to the matter at hand. Jordan and me. Me and Jordan. This thing that was totally happening between us. But I could hardly remember anything Sut *had* told me about her cousins. Except that they were visiting and from Canada. I'd mostly checked out after that.

"So, how long are you in town?" I asked.

His eyes found mine, dark and pensive. "We leave tomorrow actually."

I frowned. That sucked. Fuck. One night. Today was all we had.

"That's unfortunate. I didn't even get to show you

around Lubbock. What have you done while you've been here?"

"Nothing," he said. "Or it feels like nothing. I went to Wright Construction, met my cousins, both sets." He shrugged noncommittally. "And I got coffee, obviously."

"Well, that just will not do."

"What is there even to do around here?" he asked, sounding dubious.

"Probably not as much as Vancouver, but we have our gems. Lakes and canyons and wineries and Texas Tech football. You're missing out."

Jordan was cut off by a cry from the pool. We whipped around at the same time to see a woman I didn't recognize push a guy into the pool.

"Julian," Jordan said, stepping forward as if he could stop it. I realized this must be his brother. So, was that also his mom?

Bu there was nothing any of us could do. Julian lost his balance and crashed forward into the watery depths. He fell nearly on *top* of Jennifer with a *huge* splash.

"Mom," Jordan said with a sigh.

But his mom just laughed at the joke. She shrugged.

Julian burst out of the water, sputtering. His

hands were on Jennifer's waist, helping her to her feet as he apologized profusely. He pulled his hands back and then put them back on her wet, naked body. I could hear his string of *I'm sorry*s from here.

"Jen! Are you okay?" I called.

Jennifer turned as red as a tomato and took a step back from him. She glanced up at me with worry on her face. "Can you check my camera?"

"You okay?"

She nodded. "Just...camera."

Right. The only thing that mattered to her. Not the hot guy who had just fallen on her.

I strode over to the lounge chair where she'd left the expensive camera wrapped in a towel. The water had gotten on the chair and part of the towel but not the camera. It had been a close call. She should have never left it out here, unattended. Thankfully, the camera was fine.

"All good," I told her, giving a thumbs up.

Her shoulders visibly relaxed. "Oh, thank god."

Then she realized that Julian was still worriedly hovering over her.

"I'll take it inside, so it won't get splashed," I told her.

"Thanks," she said, backing a step from Julian.

I headed back to Jordan. "I have to take this inside for Jennifer. It's practically irreplaceable."

"I'll go with," he said. He nodded his head to the side as if to say he'd follow me. "She's a photographer?"

We fell into step as we crossed the lawn up to the house. "I wish she were. More hobby than professional. One day, I hope she takes the plunge."

"And you? What do you like to do for fun?"

I pulled open the back door, and we entered. "Well...you saw me having fun."

"True," he said, his gaze dropping to my lips before pulling back up to my eyes.

We stepped into the guest bedroom, where everyone's stuff had been deposited. The room was suddenly heated as he took another step closer to me. All the air had been sucked out of the room. I swallowed, feeling off-kilter. Something had shifted with that one step into the room. I'd been the aggressor, pursuing him at the bar and asking him out. Then approaching him here at the pool party in front of his entire family.

But the dynamic had done a one-eighty. He was in charge here, and I could feel the undercurrent pulsing between us. The way he held himself, the curve of those lips, and those eyes drinking me in.

"Are you still going out tonight?" he asked, his hand moving to my hair.

I shivered as he twirled it around his finger and then released it, brushing my shoulder.

"Yes." I reached for that effortless, flirtatious Annie that I used like a weapon. I sank into a hip and smiled. "Are you coming with me?"

"I think I will."

The way he'd said that made me tremble. I had a feeling we weren't talking about going to a bar any longer. And I was totally into it. It'd been a long time since a guy had been able to make me feel like this.

At first, I'd been glad that he was only here for one more night. My final summer fling before I started medical school. But now, looking at that face and feeling the way my stomach did flip-flops, I wasn't sure it would be that easy.

Jordan Wright might actually be a match for me.

5

JORDAN

"Hey, Jordan. Have you seen my cell phone? I don't know how I always lose the goddamn thing," Julian said as he entered my room of the hotel suite we'd gotten for the week we were in Lubbock.

"I haven't seen it."

I really didn't understand how he lost everything. As if he just couldn't fathom the responsibility. This was his third phone this year. If he lost this one, I was going to get him something that would attach to his skin.

Julian came to a stop and furrowed his brow. "What are you doing?"

"Getting dressed."

"Obviously," Julian muttered. "But why are you

getting dressed up? Aren't we just going over to Jensen's?"

"You and Mom are. I have other plans."

"What other plans? Since when?"

I finished buttoning up my white shirt and started in on rolling up the sleeves. It was hot as fuck in Texas in August. It probably would have been better to go with a breathable T-shirt, but I wasn't a T-shirt guy. Definitely not on a date.

"I have a date."

Julian glared at me. "A date? Seriously?"

"Yeah. So what?"

"So what? You're leaving tomorrow. You're going to break this poor girl's heart and never come back."

I nearly rolled my eyes at him. Julian, the romantic. Julian, who just looked at a girl and was suddenly in a three-year relationship with her. We were opposites in that regard. Well, in a lot of ways. I'd had relationships, but I'd never been good at them. They always fell apart in my hands.

But Annie was different. She didn't seem the type of girl to fall apart when I left. In fact, she'd perked up when she found out I was leaving. She was gorgeous and smart and funny. She was *exactly* what I needed after this hell of a week in Lubbock.

"I'm not you. We're just going to have fun," I told

him. "Anyway, I saw you flirting with that girl in the pool."

He crossed his arms. "Yeah. So? You talking to this girl is shitty because you're leaving and never coming back. It'd be fine for me because I'm moving here in a month."

I winced at the way he'd said it. I still couldn't get used to the idea that my mom and Julian were moving all the way to Texas.

"You're staying in Vancouver," he reminded me.

"It's not a big deal," I said. I did not want to have this conversation again.

Julian followed me out of the hotel room and into the living space. "Is this about Missy?"

"No," I said roughly. "Missy and I broke up."

"Did you though?

"Yes?"

"It didn't sound like a break up."

I narrowed my eyes at him. "The relationship was going nowhere. As it had been for the last six months. Even if this *is* about Missy, what the fuck does it matter? If I want to have some fun while I'm on my *one* vacation a year, then I'm going to have some fun."

"Do you really need a Texas rebound though?

Especially since you're not even sure if you broke up?"

I ran a hand back through my hair. "I *know* that we broke up, okay? We both needed space. That's a break up."

"Fine," Julian grumbled. "But there's another option to the rebound, you know?"

"Here it comes," I groaned.

"You could always move here *with us*," he said, spreading his arms out. "Then you could just *date* someone here."

"You know that I can't move here."

"No, I don't know that," Julian spat. He grabbed my shoulder and wrenched me around to look at him. "Mom has cancer."

"I know."

"She's getting specialty treatment here. I'll be around, but what if something happens? What if you're in Vancouver when it does?"

"I don't want to talk about this. My life is in Vancouver. That's home. I can't just pack up and move."

I wanted to be here for my mom. I wanted to figure out a way to help her, but there was no way to help her. Not by me moving all the way across the world to do it and leaving everything I knew behind.

"Your life?" Julian laughed. "What life? You mean, work? Because Wright Construction is right here."

"That's different, and you know it."

Julian shook his head. "I don't think that I do."

"Look, you and Mom made the choice to move here. You did it without even consulting me and then expect me to jump at the chance. I've always taken care of you, Julian. I'd still do it here if I could, but I can't. I'm head of the company there. That position is *filled* here. I have friends there. I have a life. It's not my fault that you're abandoning yours to move here."

"Your priorities are seriously fucked," Julian said and then stomped away.

Our mom stuck her head out of the room and looked between me and Julian's retreating back. "Hey, honey."

"Hi, Mom."

"Everything all right?"

I released the tension I'd been carrying from the same argument I'd been having with Julian for weeks. "He's still mad that I'm not moving with you two."

"Well, I'm not mad, but I am sad. I wish you

33

would come. I feel like I just got you back from your father."

"I know."

Our father was a manipulative asshole, who had turned us against our mother for years. It had taken so much time to rebuild what he'd destroyed. Even though he had been the one lying to us all along.

She touched my shoulder. "You'll do great, no matter what you decide. I don't hold it against you, like your brother does, and he'll settle down. I know he will."

"I wish that I could be here for your treatment."

She waved her hand at me, brushing the comment aside. "It'll be fine. The hospital is well-equipped to take care of me. But just because moving back to Lubbock is the right choice for me doesn't mean it is for you." She patted my arm twice. "Now, have fun on your date."

I laughed. "Did you hear our entire conversation?"

"More or less." My mom winked. "Is it the cute redhead from the party?"

"Yeah. Annie."

"She's much too pretty for you."

I snorted. "I'll keep that in mind. You're so uplifting."

"Hey, have to keep your ego in check. If you always thought you were hot shit, then your head would be too big for your shoulders."

"Appreciate it," I said with an eye roll.

"Call if you need a ride home," she said, wandering after Julian. "And remember to take condoms."

I groaned. My mother. Dear God!

With one more glance in Julian's direction, I called an Uber and headed to the address Annie had texted me. She'd said that the party had moved from Walkers to a vineyard with a stage for live music.

The Uber driver gave me a side-eye that I didn't understand until we pulled up to West Texas Winery.

"Oh," I muttered, leaning forward to catch a glimpse of the property.

Where the hell had Annie brought me?

"This is your stop," the Uber driver said.

He pulled up in front of a ramshackle barn that looked like it might collapse at any second. The vineyard behind it at least looked sustainable, based on my experience of drinking my way through Napa. That was what I thought of when I heard the word *winery* and *vineyard* in the same sentence.

Not...this.

I stepped out of the Uber, making sure to give a generous tip for driving me out into the middle of nowhere, and then stared at the dilapidated exterior. Hopefully, this wasn't the part where I got murdered.

"You here for Caprock Crew?" an unenthusiastic cowboy asked, tipping his hat at me.

"Uh...yes?"

"They just got onstage. Beers are two dollar Tuesdays." The man looked me up and down. "You prepared to get those fancy shoes dirty?"

I looked down at my shoes. They weren't even that fancy. I'd brought them with me in case I had to work...which I had. "Why am I getting them dirty?"

The man laughed, a full-belly thing, and then kicked the barn door open. "After you."

I arched an eyebrow but entered regardless and immediately understood what he'd meant.

The floor was...dirt.

And mud from where drinks had already spilled.

Everyone inside was wearing cowboy boots and hats, pressed jeans, and large belt buckles. I could not have been more out of place.

Then I found Annie waving at me from the dance floor. Her smile split her face, and she was easily the most gorgeous person in the room. Her red hair was wild as she finished some intricate footwork in her cowboy boots. She had on high-waisted jean shorts that her ass hung out of and a crop top that showed an inch of her stomach.

And just like that, my apprehension about the location dissipated.

I was here for her.

This stunning, incomparable redhead.

6

ANNIE

With a final flourish, I finished off the dance and stepped off the dusty floor. My friends tried to call me back out for the next song, but I waved them off. Jordan had walked inside a minute ago and was still staring apprehensively around the barn.

I probably should have warned him.

Okay, I definitely should have warned him.

West Texas Winery was about the shittiest locale in Lubbock. Apparently, a decade ago, it had been *the* place to go, but the owners had fallen into financial trouble, and everything had gone downhill. It'd chased away the higher-end clientele they had been going for, but the college crowd didn't seem to mind. We came here for cheap drinks and when they could get halfway decent bands to play. Tonight, they'd actually managed Caprock Crew. Albeit not the best band, they had a good beat, and the place was already packed.

A lot of the local line-dancing groups were out in force. I knew enough to get by, but they made it look like an art form.

I dashed across the barn and right up to Jordan with a smile. "You made it!"

"Yeah. The Uber driver gave me a funny look when I told him where I was going, but I made it."

"That driver doesn't know what he's missing."

Jordan's gaze swept the barn one more time, taking it all in. He still looked apprehensive.

"I probably should have told you what to wear."

"Honestly, I doubt I have anything that would make me fit in here," he admitted with a shrug. His eyes glimmered as they trailed back to me. At least he was taking it in stride.

"Well, you look great," I told him honestly.

Because he did look hot as fuck. Dress pants and a white button-up with those same fancy shoes. His hair was all gelled, and there was a soft hue of pink across his cheeks from the pool earlier.

He just didn't look like he belonged in a barn in West Texas.

"I feel ridiculous," he admitted with a laugh.

"Psh," I said, taking his arm and pulling him away from the entrance. "It's just a Texas dance party. You do know how to line dance, don't you?"

"I'm from *Vancouver*."

I snorted. "We can get you some boots," I teased playfully. "That'll help."

He shook his head. "I think I'll pass. Tell me this place has alcohol. I'm going to need to drink more for this."

"Thank God, yes."

I grinned and drew him toward the bar. I liked that he was a little out of his element here. We could have gone back to Walkers, like yesterday, but I'd wanted Jordan to try something new. He'd been here a week, and he'd hardly seen anything in Lubbock. Not that there was a ton to see, but there was more than Wright Construction. That was for sure.

"They used to only serve their wine, which is actually surprisingly good. But when they were having money problems, they got a full bar. It brings in more people."

"Interesting. I don't think I've ever seen a winery like this, and I've seen a lot of wineries."

"We can go somewhere else," I offered. I had known that this was going to be a culture shock for him, but I'd wanted to bring him anyway. Maybe it was a test. "I thought you'd want the whole experience."

He leaned against the bar, taking my hand and pulling me closer to him. "You're here. That's all I need."

I flushed all over. I wanted to reply with something flirtatious, but really, I had no words. I wasn't used to guys who were as outgoing as I was or who knew how to charm a snake. Typically, I was more than most guys could handle, and they made that known rather quickly. There was only one other guy who had been able to deal with all of *this*. Jordan surprised me.

He ordered a drink and got me another beer. I was already a little tipsy, but a beer wouldn't put me over the edge. I didn't want to be as drunk as I had been last night. Cézanne had told me that she'd dropped me off at my place, but contrary to popular belief, I didn't like not remembering how I'd gotten home. I was going to want to remember everything about tonight.

I took a sip of my beer, and then a hand clamped down on Jordan's shoulder. "Well, look what the cat dragged in."

My eyes widened at the giant of a guy who had his

hand on Jordan. Hollin Abbey was tall and broad with shoulders for days. He was older than me and had gone to a different high school. We hadn't hung in the same circles, but I still knew who he was. He worked at the winery. It didn't explain why he was touching Jordan.

But when Jordan turned around, cool as ever, his face lit up. He stuck his hand out. "Hollin!"

"Hey, Jordan! Didn't expect to find you here."

"Didn't expect to be here myself."

My eyes widened. "And how exactly do you know someone in Lubbock? You've only been here a week!"

Jordan laughed and gestured to Hollin. "This is my cousin."

I looked back at him blankly. "But...you're a Wright."

"Cousin on the other side," Hollin chimed in. He held his hand out to me now. "Hollin Abbey. It's Annie, right?"

"Yeah. We've met. So how are you two related?"

"He's my uncle's kid," Jordan told me. "We met earlier this week. I didn't expect to see him out."

Hollin shrugged and ran a hand back through his sandy-blond hair. "I'm actually the manager here."

"Here?" Jordan asked in surprise.

"Yeah, I help run the winery. The college crowd isn't always here, and you'd be shocked to learn it cleans up pretty nicely on the weekends for tours and the like. The wine is great. I'd recommend it."

"Huh," Jordan said. "You're right. I wouldn't have guessed that."

Hollin laughed. "Yeah, it's not the best on two-dollar Tuesday, I admit."

"It does clean up," I confirmed.

But Hollin was looking elsewhere. A fight had broken out on the other end of the bar. He shot us a pained expression. "If you'll excuse me, I should handle that. Tell the bartenders that Hollin sent you and get some drinks on the house."

"You don't have to do that," Jordan insisted.

"Hey, it's not every day that my cousin walks into my bar."

Jordan shook his head, but Hollin was already disappearing into the crowd, ready to pull apart the catfight. When Jordan slid his gaze back to me, I couldn't help but give him a sidelong look.

"Only here a week, huh?"

"Hollin is family. That's what I'm here for. Plus, he's giving us free drinks. So, hey, worth it."

I leaned forward against his chest, looking up into those big brown eyes. "Definitely."

Just then the band went from one song to the next, and I gasped.

"What?"

"I love this song," I said, bouncing up and down. "And I know the dance."

"The dance?"

I grinned devilishly. "You didn't think we just came here to drink, did you?"

7

JORDAN

*T*hat was exactly what I'd thought.

I had no intention of dancing. I *could* dance in the more generic terms of most dudes' ability to dance. But I wasn't from around here, and I had no idea what they were doing out on the dance floor. The most line dancing I'd ever seen done was the Electric Slide at a friend's wedding. I'd been drunk, and I still hadn't participated in that.

There was an entire troupe dipping and spinning and kicking out on the floor. I was a confident guy, but I knew my limits. Line dancing was definitely a limit.

But fuck, she looked so happy. Like she couldn't wait to get me out on that dance floor and show off her moves. So, I followed her away from the bar and into a corner, where a group of her friends hooted and hollered at her to join them.

She waved at them but turned all of her considerable attention to me. When she looked at me like that, I wanted to crush her to me and capture those perfect lips. I'd heard other girls say that confidence was a turn-on when describing me. I wasn't sure that I'd ever used it to describe a woman. Not until Annie.

No wonder I was in a dirty barn in the middle of nowhere.

"Stand here," she said, moving me into position at her side.

"What exactly are we doing?" I asked.

"I'm going to show you how to do the dance."

My brows rose. "This does not seem wise."

She laughed. Her halo of red waves bounced as her body rocked to the music. "It'll be fine. It's really easy. Promise."

"Uh..."

"This one is my favorite. You're going to love it."

I had some doubts about that. I didn't just look out of place in this barn. I *was* out of place. Even the guys were jumping in to do the dance. I straightened my shoulders and listened to her as she spouted the directions, showing me the moves at what she must have thought was a slow enough speed for me to pick them up.

"You were a cheerleader, right?"

She glanced up at me. "Yeah?"

"So, you're good at dancing."

"Pom," she said with a shrug.

"Pom?"

She giggled. "Pom is what we do in the South. Well, you probably have pom dance in Canada, but we have pom competition teams." She did a few structured arm movements, and I realized she was trying to explain that cheerleading arms were a whole dance style now.

"I have no experience with this," I said, gesturing around us.

Her eyes glittered with mirth. "I didn't think you'd have any experience. That's why I brought you. I thought you'd have fun."

And I was having fun. Completely out of my element, but I hadn't smiled this much in...years. She brought it out of me. Even while I was simultaneously more uncomfortable than I'd been in years.

"Okay," I said with a nod. "Let's try this again."

She went back to being the patient teacher. Kick right, left, right, left. Cross leg forward, hit your foot. Cross leg backward, hit your foot. Turn to face the other direction. We were going at half-speed compared to everyone else in the place, but I was kind of getting the hang of it, and her million-watt smile kept me going.

"Now, speed it up!" Annie called and fell instantly in step with the troupe of dancers.

I chuckled and held my hands up. "I can't keep up."

"Come on!" she urged. "You were doing so well."

But I took a step out of the group of dancers and gave in to defeat. I'd had it slower, but to tempo was beyond me, and that was fine. Shockingly, I was out of breath. I ran five miles a day and lifted weights, but five minutes of dancing could leave me winded. Guessed no one was in shape for all forms of exercise.

The music switched from her favorite song to the next, and she continued dancing. Her breathing was even, and she didn't seem at all out of breath. Her boots were dirty, hair flying, smile wide.

Oh fuck.

What had I gotten myself into?

I'd told Julian that I was here to have fun. That Annie had no reason to worry. I was the king of heartbreak, but I'd never thought there was any chance of that happening here. Annie wasn't interested in anything more. Plus, I was leaving tomorrow.

Still, I hadn't anticipated this...her.

She saw me gawking at her from the side of the barn. Her eyes heated. I wondered what she saw on my face. Because I wasn't hiding what I was thinking —at all. I wanted her. Not just because I'd come out to this barn for her or line-danced for her. I wanted someone that vibrant in my life. Someone who set the room on fire.

Annie slid out of the group of dancers and stepped up to face me. Her breath came out in a small pant. "We don't have to do this. We can go back to the bar. I just thought..."

I stepped into her space, tilting her chin up to look at me. Her eyes widened, and she fell silent.

"I'm right where I want to be."

She swallowed, challenge in her eyes. "Oh yeah? You like to watch me dance?"

"I think I could watch you do anything."

She bit her lip, and I contemplated sucking it into my mouth.

Fuck. *Fuck.*

"Anything?"

I nodded crisply, wrapping my arm around her waist and pulling her tight against me. "Anything.

Write grocery lists, mow the lawn, organize your bookshelves."

She laughed, bright and unexpected. "And here I thought, you were being sexy."

"I was. Mowing the lawn is sexy."

She snorted, covering her mouth with her hand. "And organizing bookshelves?"

"Definitely. Reading is sexy."

"You're...not what I thought you'd be."

"What did you expect?"

"I don't know," she admitted softly. "You're just different."

"Or maybe we're the same," I suggested, threading our fingers together.

She looked up at me with surprise, as if she'd had the same thought and not voiced it. Being here with her felt right. Normally, I'd try to play it cool, but she sliced right through that.

There wasn't playing it cool with Annie. There was just us.

And somehow, that was a relief.

8

ANNIE

I'd been to West Texas Winery more times than I could count. I'd seen it in its early glory. I'd seen it empty as they struggled when the money started to run out. I'd seen it packed, like it was tonight, as they pivoted to a more traditional bar scene.

But I'd never seen it disappear.

Not while I was inside of it.

Standing there with Jordan, the dancing, music, lights, and all the people just ceased to exist. We were on the periphery of it all, and I was trapped in that dark chocolate gaze, falling deeper and deeper into the amber flecks around the ebony pupil. Put into a trance by a vacuum into space that seemed to

51

suck us into its vortex, leaving everything else behind.

Jordan Wright had seen right into my heart and plucked out the words I'd been thinking since the pool party.

We were the same.

Somehow. Impossibly.

His hand slid down my back. My breath hitched as he passed over the inch of exposed skin before settling on my hip. I stepped into him. The pulse of energy crackled.

I'd wanted Jordan the moment I laid eyes on him, but something else was happening, and I was helpless to stop it. Even if I wanted to...which I didn't. We were barreling forward, heedless of disaster.

My eyes dipped to his lips and then back up. Oh God, those lips. I imagined all the ways they could touch my body, and the heat between us only grew. My heartbeat sped up as he drew figure eights into my skin.

"Jordan..." I whispered.

But he didn't let me finish. He swept his hands up into my hair, drawing my lips to his. I gasped at the sheer confidence in that touch. The way he held me in place without hesitation. Just grabbed me and dropped his mouth onto mine. He tasted like sweet sin. His lips were soft and tender. They pushed and pulled and devoured. Everything those deep, dark eyes had promised was found in that one press of his lips against mine.

A moan escaped me, and I slipped my arms around his neck, desperate to get closer. For more. For *him*.

His tongue brushed against mine, testing, teasing. A shiver ran down my body as all thought fled, except this precise moment in existence. He sucked my bottom lip into his mouth, and my eyes fluttered open long enough to see the self-satisfied look on his face.

I couldn't even be mad. I wanted this. I wanted that goddamn self-satisfied look. I wanted it all.

It wasn't me at all. Usually, if a guy was too into me, I got bored. If a guy thought he was too hot, I got bored. If a guy ever looked at me like *that*, I was already over it and moving on. And somehow, none of that bothered me with Jordan's mouth on mine and his body grinding against me as if at any second, he might shred my clothing.

Jordan was into me, and fuck me, but he was pleased with himself for getting me turned on. I was here for it. Like I never had been before. My brain was short-circuiting as he kissed a trail down my neck, nipping at the sensitive spot.

"Oh God," I said, barely loud enough for him to hear over the music.

I should stop this. We were in public, and while the winery wasn't well lit, it wasn't pitch-black either. Like other places, where no one much cared if you were near to fucking on the dance floor. I had a shred of decency telling me this needed to stop...or at least, we needed to take this somewhere else.

"Hey," Jordan said, drawing back to meet my gaze.

My breaths were coming out even harder than when I'd been dancing. Everything felt too hot, too close, too much., and still I didn't pull back. I didn't let him go. I had to stop myself from demanding another kiss just like that. Because I'd never forget a kiss that left me utterly breathless.

"Why don't we get out of here?" he suggested.

I nodded without hesitation. "That's a good idea."

He took my hand in his and pressed his lips to it. I leaned forward, wanting nothing more than one more of those kisses.

"Your place, or...?"

Right. He was here on vacation. He was probably

sharing a hotel with his mom and brother. I hadn't considered any of that. Frankly, I hadn't considered much, except that he was into me and I wanted to know more about him. But now, I realized that this was going to mean going to my place.

I never took guys to my place.

It was an unwritten rule between me and Jennifer.

Besides the fact that it made her uncomfortable, I'd always been the kind of girl who liked an escape route. So that there was no question of who was staying and I could skip out at any part of the process. Having a guy in *my* place felt...disruptive at best. Dangerous at worst.

And yet, I found myself nodding. Because *not* having Jordan Wright in my house was inconceivable. He absolutely was coming back with me.

Strangely, I even wanted him there.

"My place is fine," I said as easily as breathing.

"All right. You sure?"

I nodded again. "So very sure."

Then I took Jordan's hand and led him out of the winery.

I was breaking all of my rules for him. And I couldn't seem to care one bit.

9

ANNIE

*B*efore I could get all the way out of the Uber, Jordan grasped my hand, tugging me back to him. I giggled and pressed a kiss to his greedy mouth. I could hear the driver grumbling from the front seat, but I didn't care. Not when Jordan could hardly keep his hands to himself.

We stumbled out of the car and hastened up the walk to the house I rented with Jennifer. I fumbled for my keys as Jordan's arms wrapped around my waist from behind. He nuzzled into my neck, trailing kisses across my shoulders.

Just as I fit the key into the lock, he whirled me around and pushed me back against the front door.

"Oh," I gasped before his lips were on mine again.

I fisted my hands into his shirt, pulling him closer and closer until I couldn't breathe. There was no space between us. Just his hands on my body and his mouth against mine and the heat that kept building to a crescendo.

"My roommate might be home," I managed to get out as he moved to kiss my neck.

"Will that be a problem?"

He flicked the button open on my shorts before slipping his hand in just beneath the waistline. I groaned deep in my throat, not wanting him to stop. In fact, I only wanted him to move further. To push all the way down and touch me where I was aching for him.

"We'll...we'll have to be quiet," I muttered.

He arched an eyebrow. That look made me bite my lip. It screamed that he wasn't planning on keeping me quiet tonight. Did I mind? Nope. Would Jennifer? Erm...oh well.

"Well, at least until we get to my room."

I groped with the handle, twisting it and letting us tumble backward into the house. From my vantage point, it appeared Jennifer was already asleep in her room with the lights off. She was one of those monsters that lived by the mantra *early to bed, early to rise*. I was as much a vampire as I could be.

Nights were where I belonged. I'd never been more grateful that we lived on opposite schedules.

He toed the door closed behind him, and I put a finger to my mouth.

"Shh," I breathed, eyeing Jen's door. Luckily, it remained closed.

But then, he was there. Our bodies tight, his mouth against my ear as he growled, "No promises."

I shivered.

I didn't think I minded that he wasn't going to be quiet. There was something about Jordan that made it all fit. Maybe it was just the straight lust building between us, but it felt like more. There was a reason that I didn't bring guys back to my place. I wasn't the kind of girl who got lost in guys. I made a lot of mistakes and I flirted outrageously and I enjoyed playing the field. But this was different. I didn't have an escape route, and I didn't even want one.

He tugged my crop top over my head, leaving me in my lacy balconette bra that did nothing to hold the girls but looked amazing as they spilled out of it. And by Jordan's reaction, it worked.

"Which room?" he asked.

I pointed down the hall as I kicked my boots off at the door. He removed his shoes just as the opposite door creaked open.

"Annie?" a voice called. "Are you home?"

I gasped and launched for my shirt, which Jordan had discarded somewhere on the floor. I scrambled to my feet with the tiny piece of material between me and Jennifer, who was standing in her doorway in sweats and an oversize T-shirt.

"Jen! I thought you were asleep," I said, overly cheerful.

Jordan had finished with his shoes and stood next to me.

"I was reading, but I heard voices." Her eyes drifted to Jordan, and then they visibly rounded. "Uh...did I interrupt?"

"No!" I said quickly. "Nothing to see here."

Jordan chuckled, and I nudged him with my elbow.

"I didn't mean to...get in the way. Sorry about that." She awkwardly waved at Jordan and squeaked, "Hi."

"How's it going?" Jordan said, completely uncon- cerned that I was half-undressed in the middle of our living room.

"Oh, fine. I'm just going to..." She gestured behind her. Her face was beet red, and she tried to find something to do with her hands. "Just, uh... forget that I was here. Have fun."

Then she rushed back into her room and shut the door.

I met Jordan's gaze, and we burst into laughter.

"Think we traumatized her?" he asked as he took the shirt from out of my hands.

"Maybe," I said. "I don't normally do this."

Not here at least.

"Mmm," he said, his hands returning to my body. "Maybe we should move this elsewhere."

I gestured toward the bedroom, but he slipped his hands down my legs, grasped my thighs, and hoisted me into the air. I squealed, throwing my arms around him. My eyes drifted over his shoulder to Jennifer's bedroom. I was going to have an interesting conversation with her tomorrow. But I was currently living for tonight.

Jordan walked us both down the hall to my bedroom. Before we got there, he thumped me back against the wall.

"Shh," I whisper-shouted.

He crushed his mouth to mine, breaking away only long enough to say, "You're not going to be asking me to keep quiet later."

"Oh God."

He kissed me again with a ferocity that made my entire body shudder.

"I can't get enough of you," he muttered, his hands slipping up my legs as he leveraged me against the wall. "I could take you right here."

I whimpered. My core pulsing at the filthy words.

His body ground against mine. The full length of him pressed hard against my tiny shorts.

My head fell backward with another thump that I couldn't bring myself to care about. Jen would fend for herself. I was too focused on the precise feel of him as he worked his hips against mine.

He'd been lying about knowing how to dance. Because if the circle of his hips was any indication, he knew what he was doing.

"Please." I didn't know what I was begging for. For him not to stop. For him to fuck me here against the wall. For it all.

"I would," he said, twisting the door open and shooting me a look of pure sin, "but I want to savor you."

There was something in Jordan's eyes when he pushed open the bedroom door and dropped me to my feet. Something even hotter than when he'd offered to fuck me right there.

"Savor me?"

"Oh yes," he said, closing the door behind us. "I'm going to take my time."

I swallowed in anticipation. I'd had one-night stands before. Not a ton, but a few. And the guys, in my experience, were interested in getting off and getting out. There was no savoring. There was no taking their time. Honestly, I hadn't done anything like this with a stranger in a long time because of that very fact. Most guys who wanted to date me weren't much better.

But here was Jordan, walking me back toward my king-size bed, decorated in soft gray and blues, and I didn't think he was blowing smoke. He wasn't just saying what I wanted to hear.

"You seem skeptical," he said.

I bit my lip. My legs hit the footboard, and I leaned back against the mattress invitingly. "No, you just seemed to be in a hurry."

"Can you blame me?".

His hands ran down my exposed stomach before dragging the zipper down my shorts, revealing the pink thong underneath. Oh God, I couldn't seem to get enough of him. He tugged me back to my feet to help me slide out of my shorts. My fingers grappled with the last few buttons of his shirt. I wrenched it back over his shoulders, and he let it drop to the floor, next to my shorts.

He'd said to take it slow, but I didn't know what

that meant. Not when I was staring at the planes of his tight stomach. The six-pack on display. I'd wanted to run my nails down every ridge at the pool but held back with self-restraint that I certainly wasn't known for. I did it now. Leaving long red marks across his abs as I worked my way downward.

His eyes glazed as I got to that glorious V that led into his pants. I trailed my hands across each line, dipping my fingers into the waistline.

He might want to savor me, but I'd never been patient. My fingers deftly unbuckled his buckle, popped the button, and pulled on the zipper. His pants hung low on his waist now, and I could see the erection prominent in the black boxer briefs. My body clenched with need.

I couldn't hold it back any longer. I slipped my hand under the material and took him in my hand.

Jordan inhaled sharply. His hands fisted into my hair, and he brought his lips down on mine. I held his dick between us, stroking him up and down as he ravaged my mouth with his. It was hot and feverish. I never wanted it to stop.

"Jordan," I groaned against his mouth.

"Fuck," was his only response.

And that was exactly how I felt. I wanted to fuck. I knew what came next. I knew the rhythm of this.

I looked up into those glassy sex eyes. He stepped forward, capturing one more kiss from me. Then I released his dick and dropped to my knees before him, taking his pants with me on the descent.

"Annie, wait..."

His hands were suddenly on my shoulders, pulling me back to my feet. I stood in surprise; the confusion must have been obvious on my face. I'd been seconds from giving him a blow job. Why in God's name had he stopped me?

"Slow down."

I laughed brittlely. "Now you want to slow down?"

"Well, no. I don't want to, and I'm not going to."

"What?"

But I received no response in words. He stopped me from going down on him, but in one fluid motion, he was on his knees before me. He slid off my thong, lifted my legs off of the ground, and spread them wide before him, like a man preparing for a challenge and my orgasm was his prize.

"Wait, I can..." I gasped out.

These weren't the steps I had expected. This almost *never* happened.

He shot me that wicked grin. "I'm going to enjoy this."

10

ANNIE

*I*f he wanted to go down on me, I wasn't planning to stop him. I'd never had a man excited to do it, only to get between my legs for a quick fuck. In fact, I'd rarely had a man give two shits about what I was getting out of this. Definitely not any who moved as fast as Jordan. Men were selfish. Unfortunately, I'd learned to live with that.

Jordan was not like other men.

He spread my lips, slicking two fingers through my wetness.

"So fucking wet," he ground out.

He ran fingers back and forth, back and forth, against the sensitive area. My body tensed and tightened as he worked me into a frenzy but didn't take that one step forward. Didn't slide those fingers in exactly where I wanted him. He really *was* going to take his time.

I whimpered, aching for more.

He chuckled. Clearly, he liked that he was driving me mad with want. But that didn't stop him from continuing to tease me with his fingers. Then when I thought I couldn't handle any more, he slipped his thumb up to the apex of my thighs. I jumped the first time he touched my clit. The sensation was so erotic that it was almost too much at once.

"Oh God," I breathed.

He eased up, removing some of the pressure but continuing to move in slow, tight circles. I shuddered all over as he stroked me into submission while his fingers.

Then his tongue replaced his finger, and I saw stars. He licked up and down with wild, rapid strokes that had me bucking off of the bed. Without missing a beat, he laid his arm across my hips, effectively pinning me in place so that he could continue.

"Jordan. Fuck. Oh fuck."

In one quick motion, he slid two fingers inside of me. I cried out, heedless of my volume. Forget all the shushing I'd been doing earlier. There was no way that I could be quiet while he took his time with me.

It only took a few strokes of my pussy while he worshipped my clit before I released. I cried out. My body pulsed relentlessly, trying to keep his fingers inside of me.

Everything went fuzzy around the edges.

He retreated, giving me a self-satisfied look. As if to say, *See, savor you.*

I couldn't even deny it. He'd done exactly that.

"Now is it my turn?" I asked, coming back to myself.

I didn't wait for an answer. I drew down his boxers and took his dick in my hand. He was somehow even bigger than when I'd first held him, and pre-cum dripped from the head. Going down on me had turned him on, and I wasn't going to waste the subsequent reaction.

I returned to my knees and licked the bead off of the tip of him. He groaned at the first lave of my tongue against him, and I was just getting started. I put the tip of him to my mouth and gradually took the rest of him all the way in.

His hand settled in my hair, holding me in place for the span of a second. "Fuck yes, Annie."

I slowly dragged backward and then took him in again. My tongue rolled around the head, and he shuddered with pleasure. I could taste the tangy saltiness of him as I worked him impossibly bigger.

Suddenly, his fist halted me. "As much as I want to watch you suck me off," he said with great strain, "I want to fuck you."

I stroked his cock as I looked up into his eyes. My heart rate was elevated, and hearing him say he wanted to fuck me was a turn-on like nothing else.

"I want to finish."

"I want you to finish," he assured me as he helped me to my feet. "I want to do this more."

He turned me around and bent me over the side of the bed. I moaned as he spread my feet wider, baring me for his display. He stroked his fingers back through my wetness. I'd never felt so...exposed. And still, I was so wet that it was dripping down the sides of my legs. I should have been embarrassed, but I couldn't find it in myself to care.

Between his dirty talk and the command in all of his gestures and the way he took control of the situation, I was a goner. I might have been the aggressor to begin with, but he had me now.

He gripped my cheeks tightly and spread them apart. I clenched all over. The waiting was sweet torture. He could have shoved right in me, and I would have taken it with pleasure. Instead, he teased me, dropping his hands back to my inner thighs and running them achingly slow up to my pussy, where he fingered me until I thought I might come again.

"Jordan, please..."

I heard the crinkle of material behind me. Good thing he was thinking ahead. My brain had short-circuited.

The head of his cock settled against my opening. I pushed back, wanting him inside of me more than anything in existence at that moment. But he held me firmly with hands on my hips to keep me from moving and settled himself at my opening.

He pushed in, and I sighed with relief when he seated himself all the way in. So deep that I could barely breathe. A slight mix of pain and pleasure heating me through.

"God, you feel so good," he said, dragging a hand down my back.

"Yes," I breathed.

Then he pulled out, and it felt nearly as good as going in. Like sweet relief. Then emptiness. And I didn't want emptiness. I wanted to be full. Full like I'd never been before in my life.

And then he thrust in so deep and hard that I saw stars. It was uncomfortable and somehow perfect. It was exactly what I'd always wanted.

We were both so close from the foreplay that I could feel myself on the edge of the abyss. My hands gripped the comforter. His held my hips steady, so he could continue to pound into me. I clenched my jaw and buried my face in the mattress. The sensations too raw, too real. My body tightened and tightened and tightened until it felt like a dam ready to burst at any second.

"Oh God," I cried.

Then I lost it. I came apart with him buried deep inside of me. I couldn't control the sounds of my shouts or the arch of my back or the vise grip I now had on his cock.

"Fuck." He thrust in me one last time before following up my orgasm with a roar so loud that my neighbors probably heard.

And I couldn't even seem to care.

Not one bit.

Not while he was still inside of me.

Not while I was lying, panting, on the bed.

Not when I'd had the best sex of my entire life.

Jordan finally withdrew. I rolled over and crawled on top of the bed, collapsing in a heap. He tossed the condom and then came to lie next to me.

Our breathing was ragged. Our arms splayed out. Our bodies recovering from the intense orgasms.

I rolled my head to the side to look back into those dark eyes. He was already looking at me. An expression like I was a siren who had bewitched him.

He reached out and brushed the loose strands of my hair out of my face, entranced. "Come here."

He shifted me into the spot against his chest with my head resting on his shoulder. I felt...secure. Like this was where I was always meant to be. A piece of the puzzle that had settled into place.

Even though it didn't make sense. This was a one-night stand. It was with a guy who was leaving tomorrow. Who I'd probably never see again. It wasn't supposed to be anything more than that. We were both into each other, so why deny the inevitable?

But then *this* had happened. The incredible sex where he knew just what I wanted and how and when. Even when I'd wanted faster and more, he had taken his time, building my climax higher and higher until I touched the clouds before coming down. This...this was something else. Something mind-blowing.

Jordan Wright had changed me. We might have only known each other for twenty-four hours, but something had shifted.

So, I said the thing I shouldn't. The thing that I should keep in my heart and lock away forever.

"I wish you were staying," I said, barely above a whisper.

And to my surprise, he kissed my head, threaded our fingers together, and said, "Me too."

11

JORDAN

The next morning, sunlight streaked in through the open blinds. I blinked awake to the unfamiliar surroundings. Then Annie's comforting weight wrapped up in my arms, fast asleep and relaxed, brought me back to the night before. I couldn't keep the smile from my face. When was the last time I'd felt this way? So...free.

I honestly couldn't remember. Missy and I had dated nearly a year, probably the longest relationship of my life, and I'd never once felt like this. It had been a constant struggle to keep up with her high-profile life and ever more ridiculous demands. There was no freedom in a life lived in manipulation.

Who knew that I'd have to come to Lubbock,

Texas—the place my father had sworn to never take me—to find even an ounce of hope?

Annie snuggled in closer. Her arm slung across my waist with her head buried in my shoulder. She sighed pleasantly as she got more comfortable.

I could stay here forever.

The thought shocked me. Shocked me enough for reality to close back in.

This wasn't my life. This was...a one-night stand with a beautiful woman. Nothing more. Nothing less. It couldn't be anything else. Not when I had a life in Vancouver and a business to run there.

I reached across the bed for my phone, where I'd left it last night on the nightstand. The screen blinked on, and the time read ten o'clock.

My eyes bulged.

Ten o'clock? Fuck.

My normal wake-up time was six. I went for my five-mile run before showering and heading into the office. I'd never in a million years thought that I'd sleep past even seven. Our flight back home was set to leave at one fifteen. Normally, that would be plenty of time, but right now, it sent me into a panic.

"Annie," I whispered, lightly shaking her awake.

Big green eyes looked up at me. She yawned and

stretched her arm overhead. "G'morning," she murmured. "What time is it?"

"Ten."

"Mmm." She snuggled even closer. "Good. Then we have a few hours before I have to be human."

I would have laughed, except that her hand was drifting lower to the waistline of my boxer briefs. "Annie...I have to go."

"Already? Are you sure?" she asked sleepily.

Her hand slipped underneath, and my cock hardened at her touch. Now, I was not sure about leaving. Not even a little. Maybe I should have left before she woke up, but I didn't want to leave, and that was the problem.

I stilled her hand. "I have a flight to catch."

Her nose moved to my ear. "It could be a quickie."

Fuck, this woman. Fuck. Where had she come from? And how was I just finding her now?

When I didn't stop her again, she took that as acquiescence. She tossed her leg over my body, straddling my hips. She wore nothing but a pink thong, her amazing tits on full display as she ground herself against me.

Well, fuck it.

I reached into the side table, where she'd

revealed a stash of condoms last night, and pulled one out. We discarded our underwear, and then she fitted the condom onto my cock, inch by inch.

I was beyond wondering whether or not this was a good idea.

Annie lifted her hips, leaning forward to brush her lips against mine, and then she aligned my cock with her opening. It was sweet torture, watching her take control. The feel of her pussy inching down over me. I couldn't take it anymore. I slammed her down hard.

She gasped. Her eyes rolled back into her head, but the word that came out of her mouth was, "Yes."

And I was a fucking goner.

I rolled her hips to reach deeper and deeper points. Then I lifted her hips and forced her back down. Over and over again. She righted her body, using her knees to help me lift and lower her. Until we were nothing but a fast rhythm of her impaling herself on my cock. And watching her tits bounce, her mouth forming into an O, and her red hair running wild, I was ready to come.

"Oh, Jordan. Fuck," she ground out. "Keep going. I'm so close."

I sat up, crushing her chest to mine. She wrapped her legs tight around my body, and I worked her harder and harder. Until she cried out, throwing her head back as her orgasm hit her. As she tightened hard around me, it triggered my own release. I tugged her even closer as I thrust one more time into her, spending every last drop.

Annie shivered for a few seconds before collapsing backward onto the bed. "Oh my God."

And it was all I could think, too. Because oh my fucking God.

I tossed the condom and cleaned up, coming back to the bedroom to find her half-asleep, still in the exact position I'd left her.

"You fucked me senseless."

I laughed as I reached for my clothes again. "You were the one who asked for a quickie."

"It was not a complaint," she said with a lascivious smirk.

Fuck, I wanted to crawl back into that bed and get her to look at me like that for all of eternity.

But I couldn't.

"I have to go."

She sighed heavily. "I know."

She didn't repeat the things we'd said last night. About how we both wished that I could stay. There was no point. I was leaving. The afterglow had faded, and only reality remained.

I finished buttoning up my shirt, and she still lay there, completely naked. It was making it very difficult to focus.

"One more time?" she whispered.

"I wish I could, love," I breathed, pressing a kiss to her swollen pink lips.

"Do you...need a ride back to your hotel?"

I shook my head. Saying good-bye to her was already too hard. I wasn't going to make it more difficult on both of us. "I'd rather imagine you still naked in bed, if I'm honest."

She laughed and pulled me down for another kiss. Her eyes said all that I needed to know. I was sure that mine mirrored that look. The one that said, *Stay.*

So, I stepped back, releasing her and all the warring thoughts in my mind. The treacherous parts that said maybe I could stay. Maybe it wouldn't be so bad if I could have this, too.

Then I remembered how I broke relationships. How they fell apart in my hands like sand in a sieve. I didn't want to break this, too. It would be better to remember this one perfect night than to wreck what could have been with what would be.

Still, I kissed her one more time before hurrying out of her room. I found my shoes where I'd left them at the entranceway and ran into her roommate, Jennifer, with a cup of coffee.

"Oh!" she gasped. "You're still here."

"Just leaving."

"She must really like you."

"Oh yeah?"

Jennifer shrugged. "She doesn't bring guys home. Not ever. It's her rule."

I stared at her in confusion. "She didn't seem concerned with bringing me back."

"Well, yeah, like I said..."

She must really like you.

Fuck. I needed to get out of here. I couldn't think about that. I was set on my course, and I had no intention of changing paths. No matter that there was a feisty redhead who made me want to throw out all of my rules, too.

"Nice meeting you," I said to Jennifer while I wrangled an Uber back to the hotel.

She waved as I left. And I tried not to think about the fact that I was leaving Annie behind.

12

JORDAN

*T*he drive to the hotel was blessedly short. I was making my first ever walk of shame. Though I felt no shame for my night with Annie. The exact opposite actually. I was light as air.

I tapped my card to enter the room and found it in chaos. Instead of the quiet judgment I'd expected to find from my mom and brother, I found that the entire suite had been taken over by Wrights. All five of my cousins were crammed into the space. Jensen speaking with my mom on the couch. Morgan and Austin seemingly embroiled in some debate with Julian. Landon had his arms crossed, a look of derision on his face, as he watched. As if he knew exactly how this would end and wanted no part of it. Sutton stood at the window, staring off into space. No one seemed to notice her clear look of distress.

It was Sutton who noticed me first. I was still in last night's clothes. My hair was freshly sex-tousled. My shoes still dirty from the barn. It was pretty obvious where I'd been and what I'd been doing.

Sutton sighed. As if she already knew exactly who I'd been out all night with. Annie was her best friend. Of course she knew.

"Hey, Jordan," she said, drawing everyone else's attention as well.

Seven sets of eyes turned to me at once. Austin smirked, and Landon smacked him when he started to make some comment about my appearance. Jensen and Morgan exchanged a look. Both had been my boss in the past. I knew what that looked like from a boss's perspective. I didn't know what it meant from my cousins.

It was my mom who broke the silence. "Jordan, so glad that you came back from getting coffee, but didn't you forget our drinks?"

I stared at her, comprehension dawning. They'd spun a story as to why I was gone. Likely why I'd missed the final Wright party thing last night. Apparently, I should have checked my messages in the ride over, or I might have known to bring coffee.

Julian clapped me on the shoulder. "So selfish. You only got yourself coffee."

"Completely slipped my mind," I said. Not that anyone seemed to believe the lie my family was spinning.

"It's fine. I'll drink the cheap stuff," Julian said, gesturing to the counter with a small coffeepot.

"Cool. I'm going to go finish packing."

Then I hastened out of the suite living space. Luckily, I'd packed almost everything last night before meeting Annie, but I'd use anything as an excuse to change.

After a quick shower and fresh clothes, I returned to the suite to talk with my cousins. They'd come over to say good-bye and once again let Julian and my mom know that they'd be happy to help with anything they needed for the move. It was an exhausting half hour before they left, except for Jensen, who had offered to drive us to the airport.

Sutton shot me an incredulous look over her shoulder before leaving. She looked like she wanted to say more, but then she left without a word. I could only guess that she was heading to Annie's place after this. Wonderful.

"So," Julian said, coming to stand at my side, "did you have a nice night?"

I knew that he was being a sarcastic shit, who didn't care about my night. He sounded irritated that I'd chosen to hang out with a random stranger rather than with him on our last night in town. I couldn't seem to care, because, yeah, I'd had a great fucking night.

I put a smile on my face. "It was amazing, actually. Thanks for asking."

Julian startled at my genuine response. He just stared at me in surprise.

Jensen broke the tension by offering his hand. "I'm glad that you came out this week, Jordan."

"So am I."

We shook.

Julian sighed. "I'm going to help Mom down to the car."

"She's not infirm," I said quickly.

Julian shot me a glare. "No, she's not. She's a fighter, but that doesn't mean that I shouldn't take care of her."

"Of course not, but..."

Julian didn't let me respond. He just stalked away.

I watched his retreating back with frustration. All the good feels I'd had this morning disappearing.

"He's still mad that I'm not moving with them," I told Jensen to add context to Julian's outburst.

"Yeah, he mentioned something about that. I can't blame him. I still sometimes get mad when I think about Landon living across the country, but it's irrational. He'll adjust."

"I know. We've just never been apart. It's always been me and Julian against the world."

Jensen nodded his head in complete understanding. He was also an older sibling. He knew what it was like to take care of others. And how hard it was to watch them live their own lives.

"Well, now you're not alone anymore."

I turned to look him in his face. One that was so similar to my own. "I'm not sure I'm used to having other family."

"Me either. When our parents died, it was just me taking care of the five younger ones. I never knew if I was doing it right or being enough for them. But it's family that gets us through, and you're family, Jordan."

"Thanks," I said with a hand back through my hair.

"I understand your decision to stay in Vancouver, but I would like to let you know that you are welcome here, just like your brother and your mom."

I nodded. I had known that. At least, I'd sort of known that.

"My life is there," I said automatically. The same argument I was giving everyone. "And I'm heading the company up there. Morgan has it handled here as far as I can tell. There wouldn't be a spot for me."

"Let me assure you that you shouldn't worry about work. I already talked to Morgan, and we both agreed that we could make room for you. You wouldn't have to trade the work that you're doing, and we wouldn't reduce your pay. We want you here. We want you to be happy here."

I stared at him in mild shock. Words I never thought would come out of his mouth. They'd just *find* a place for me. As if it were that easy. But maybe it was. Maybe they'd restructure so that I had a spot, doing what I loved. I wouldn't be at the head of a company, but I wouldn't be lost in the dregs either.

"It almost sounds too good to be true."

"Family first," Jensen said, offering his hand again.

I took it. "What's Wright is right, huh?"

Jensen laughed at my reiteration of the company motto. "Exactly. You should think about it."

I *had* thought about it. And every time, it felt impossible. Leaving everything behind to move to a new country with family that I barely knew and a place I had no idea whether or not I'd ever learn to love.

Then a certain redhead popped into my vision, and that freedom settled over me again. That sense that I had a choice, and I could do anything. Even move to Lubbock...

13

ANNIE

*a*fter Jordan left, I must have fallen back asleep because I woke again with a start when someone banged on my door.

"Annie, Sutton's here," Jennifer called.

I stretched and yawned again. "All right. I'll get up."

Jennifer huffed. I could hear her disdain through the door. "You're still asleep? It's nearly eleven."

"And?"

I was going to have to change my schedule up once I started school, but why would Jennifer want to force me out of my happy place on one of my last days of freedom? I rolled off the bed and found a pair of shorts and a tank. I wrenched the door open to find Jennifer smirking at me.

Her gaze drifted to my destroyed bedroom. "Late night?"

"I can neither confirm nor deny."

Then I shouldered past her and into the living room. Sutton was seated in a chair with a cup of coffee in her hand, staring out the back window into our tiny backyard.

"Morning," Sutton said.

"Hey." I stifled a yawn and went to pour myself a cup of coffee. I flopped down on the couch across from her. "What's up? Where's Jason?"

"He's with his grandparents," she told me.

"Cool. To what do I owe the pleasure of your visit?"

She looked at me finally, a small smile tugging on her lips. "As if you don't know."

I laughed and shrugged. "I mean, I know, but how do you already know? Did Jennifer tell you?"

Jennifer sank into another seat and shook her head. "I wouldn't break your confidence like that."

Sutton rolled her eyes. "She should have told me, but for one, I already guessed at the pool party when you were all up in Jordan's business. And two, I saw him come back to his hotel, doing a very convincing walk of shame. After his mom and brother tried to tell us he'd gone out for coffee. Of course, he came back without coffee."

"Whoops," I said with a mischievous grin.

"Why am I not even surprised that you had a one-night stand with my cousin?"

"Because she's Annie," Jennifer said.

"Hey!" I muttered, flinging a pillow in her direction.

"Precisely," Sutton said.

"Just because neither of *you* are getting any doesn't mean that I shouldn't!"

Jennifer's cheeks heated a bright red. Sutton just flinched slightly. Maybe that hit a little too close to home.

"I didn't mean—"

"It's fine," Sutton said at once. "But did it have to be my cousin?"

Of course, it didn't have to be her cousin. But it was. It was a hundred percent Jordan. A slow smile touched my lips. One I couldn't even seem to control. We'd had a perfect night and, beyond that, a perfect morning. I'd wanted everything that happened. I'd shocked myself into admitting that I wanted more.

I couldn't have more though. Obviously, he was going back home today, and I was starting medical school. I'd have no time for anything. Let alone a guy who lived in a different country.

I sighed, letting the smile disappear. It was fun while it lasted.

"Wait," Sutton said. "Do you actually like him?"

"What? No," I said at once.

Jennifer arched an eyebrow.

I set my mug down and shrugged. "Okay, maybe a little. We were really good together, but it was just one night. We both knew that. A one-night stand to send him home to Vancouver. It's not like I'll ever see him again."

Sutton looked alarmed.

"What?" I asked in confusion. "Why are you looking at me like that?"

"Did you two talk last night when you were together or just..." She left the end of the question implied.

"We talked some," I said defensively. "Why? What am I missing? He's going back to Vancouver, right?"

"Yes," she said quickly. "But how could you think you'd never see him again when his brother and mom are moving here in a month?"

I nearly sprayed the coffee from my mouth. "They're doing *what*?"

"I don't know how you missed that," Jennifer said. "They announced it at the pool party."

I scoured my brain for that information, but no, I must not have been there when they announced it, and Jordan hadn't told me. Maybe he'd thought I already knew?

"But...but why are they moving here?"

Sutton looked down, clenching her mug with a white-knuckled grip. "Their mom has cancer. She's coming here for treatments."

"Oh, Sut," I whispered.

So much loss in her life. She wouldn't handle any more of it well.

"It's fine," she said simply. "They're moving here for treatments. I guess she's always wanted to move back, but she didn't want to leave her kids."

"And Julian is moving with her?"

Sutton nodded.

"But not Jordan?"

"As far as I know...no. But he's going to visit. His mom and brother are moving here, and she has cancer. He's going to be here, Annie."

"Fuck," I whispered.

"I'm pretty sure they're coming to Jensen and Emery's wedding next month."

My eyes widened. Why hadn't Jordan told me

any of this? Not that I'd expected much from a one-night stand, but a part of me had thought—unrealistically—that this was more. I didn't know when it had happened last night. But it felt almost like...fate had brought us together. Then when I'd woken up and seen him leave, I'd tried to convince myself that it didn't matter.

And now, here was the proof that I'd been right.

Because if Jordan Wright hadn't told me that he'd be back, then he hadn't wanted me to know. Which made me the one-night stand that I'd been telling myself I wasn't.

"It's fine," I said instantly. "Why should I care?"

"Annie..."

"Seriously, Sut, it's cool. It was a one-night stand. He'll visit, but it's not a big deal. It's not like *he's* moving here."

"But I thought you were into him."

"I was, but I'm starting medical school. You know I won't have time for anything. Jordan was a fun... and that's all."

The lie must have been convincing because my friends moved on to different topics. Sutton's issues with David and Jennifer's upcoming pharmacy applications and the wedding she'd been asked to be a second shooter for.

I sat back and let the conversation wash all around me.

Jordan was going to be in town to see his mom and brother. He clearly hadn't wanted me to know that. So, while last night might have been the best sex of my life and I might have said something outrageous about wanting him to stay, he didn't actually feel that way.

It was just a one-night stand.

It wasn't like I'd fallen in love with him.

Right?

TO BE CONTINUED

ACKNOWLEDGMENTS

Thank you so much for reading One Wright Stand! I hope you enjoyed this prequel to Annie & Jordan's story which continues in Wright with Benefits. Turn the page to read a sneak peek into the next book!

I can't thank enough people for their dedication to the Wright family and the ability to continue to write in this universe. I never knew moving to Lubbock, TX would be so fruitful. So thank you to all the readers who made this possible, my husband Joel for listening through all of my plotting shenanigans, and all the people in my life and on my team who made this possible!

WRIGHT WITH BENEFITS

CHAPTER ONE — ANNIE

A brisk wind whipped around my bare legs, swirling the skirt of my black dress and flipping it upward, Marilyn Monroe–style. I shrieked, batting at the material in a desperate attempt to bring it back down to an acceptable length. The wind didn't seem to hear my string of curses because it just bit into me harder, making me regret forgoing tights.

"Oh my God," I snapped as I clutched the material in my hands.

The wind whistled in response. A cackle if I'd ever heard one.

I glared up at the stupid Lubbock wind. It wasn't enough that the temperatures were in the low thirties already at five thirty on this Friday afternoon right before my last semester of medical school started; the wind had to rub it in.

"Annie, why are you standing out here?" Cézanne asked. She wore a black jumpsuit that highlighted her dark brown skin with her box braids pulled up into a high ponytail. She somehow looked professional and like an imperious, avenging angel. "It's below freezing."

I prayed to the Lord for patience and grinned at my closest friend in my cohort. "The wind attacked me."

She eyed me skeptically. We'd known each other pre–med school, and she still sometimes looked at me like I'd sprung a second head.

I waved her off. "Whatever. I'm not having a good day."

Which was an understatement. My house had *flooded*! Like, straight flooded. My room was a wreck. I'd lost half of my closet, including *all* of my shoes. Like, every pair, except the impossibly high snake-skin heels that I'd scrounged out of a pile of donations I hadn't gotten rid of yet. My room was essentially awash until maintenance showed up. I'd be living on the couch for the foreseeable future.

If that hadn't been bad enough, I'd been nearly run off the road on the way here. Some dipshit had driven straight through a red light, and I'd had to swerve to avoid getting T-boned.

Today was officially over.

I stepped inside the rustic building the medical school had rented for the event, and Cézanne closed the door.

"Well, if you've been having a bad day, I hate to ask, but where's the wine?" Cézanne asked warily.

"What wine?"

"The...wine. You know, the case of commemorative wine for Professor Rodgers and the rest for the retirement party. The entire school is coming, and... there's no wine."

"What the hell? Who was in charge of that?"

Cézanne looked at me blankly.

"No," I told her.

"It has your name next to it."

I shook my head. "I swear I wasn't in charge of the wine."

She passed the list to me, and I saw where my name was scrawled unintelligibly. I groaned.

"Are you sure it was even called in? I didn't do it."

"I'm not sure who called it in, but I have the original order request."

"Let me see it."

I plucked it out of her hand and stared down at

it. Phew! It was three thousand dollars' worth of wine. The commemorative case alone was a grand. Well, no wonder Cézanne was wondering where the hell all the wine was.

Unfortunately, it didn't say who had put the order in. But I knew for a fact that it wasn't me.

I took a deep breath and then released it. "How can I help?"

Cézanne grinned. "Can you please call the Wine Boutique and find out what happened?"

"Yeah, I can do that."

"Thank you. Thank you. I knew I could count on you to get shit done."

I sighed. What else could possibly make this day worse? Might as well try to get the wine, so we could all get fucked up today. Professor Rodgers was only retiring once.

Cézanne checked off a slot on her to-do list that rested on an actual clipboard. I loved Cézanne to death, but sometimes, her organizational skills were so extra. There was a reason she was top of our class and in charge of all of our events.

I stepped away from Cézanne to make my phone call. The Wine Boutique's number was on the top of the order, and I dialed it with another sigh. This was what I got for being dependable. The line rang and rang and rang. It felt like an eternity before the voicemail clicked over.

"Thank you for calling the Wine Boutique. Sorry we missed your call…"

I hung up and tried again. And again. And again. No answer.

Their hours said that they were open until six. I had another thirty minutes. They should have answered their phone.

"Gah!" I growled, wanting to throw my useless phone across the room.

Of course no one was answering. It was just my day. I checked the address on the sheet again. I knew where this place was. It was only a five-minute drive downtown on a good day. Today was not a good day, but I had enough time to still make it.

"Cézanne!" She glanced over at me. "No one is answering. I'm going to head over there and find out what happened."

"You're a goddess, Annie. Truly."

"I still say that I wasn't in charge of this."

"Well, find out who was then, 'kay?"

"Yeah, yeah," I muttered as I headed back outside.

I braced myself against the cold and hustled back to my car. As soon as I shut myself back inside, I blasted the heat. The Spirit Ranch was a wedding venue on the north side of town that we'd gotten at an uber discount since it was the off-season. But Cézanne had somehow still made the space look gorgeous, even going as far as renting an outdoor tent, complete with heaters. But with the sun already going down, I couldn't imagine standing out there. Maybe with enough alcohol in me.

I winced.

Right...alcohol. That thing we didn't have.

With a groan, I peeled away from the building and headed toward downtown. The Wine Boutique was nestled in the heart of the city between an old city hall and a historic hotel, which had recently been renovated into high-end apartments. Downtown was finally—*finally*—beginning to blossom into the Lubbock local scene that everyone had always hoped for. It had a long way to go, but I could see where it was headed.

I parked out front, bracing myself for the cold, and rushed toward the front door. My hand settled on the gilded doorknob, and I yanked on the door. I groaned, feeling my shoulder give as I pulled too hard on a door that wouldn't budge.

"Fuck," I spat.

The hours on the front door said I had another

fifteen minutes before they closed—because, of course, it had taken me longer to get here. I peered inside at the darkened interior. A few lights were still on, and a woman sat behind the counter, typing on the computer.

I banged on the front door. "Hello!"

The woman's head popped up in confusion. Then she dashed across the room, unlocked the door, and threw it open. I nearly fell inside.

"Hey! Sorry about that. I didn't expect any other customers," the woman said. She wore a blue dress with sensible heels. Her brown hair was severely parted down the middle and pulled back into a bun. Her lips were painted a pretty pink, and her dark eyes were lightly lined.

"Not a problem."

"I'm the owner, Sophia. How can I help you?"

"Annie," I said, taking her outstretched hand and shaking it. "I'm actually here from the medical school. We're hosting a retirement party for one of our distinguished faculty up at the Spirit Ranch today. We ordered a few cases of wine from here, but it was never delivered."

I passed over the order form to Sophia, who looked even more surprised when she scanned it over.

"I have this order," she said, "but it's for next weekend."

"No, it's for today. We're all back in rotations next weekend."

"I don't even have to look it up. I know that I have it for next weekend."

Sophia immediately went to the computer. I followed her, standing before the desk. She quickly printed out a similar form and passed it to me.

I glanced down at it. It was nearly identical to the draft form I'd handed her, except that the date was filled in on the completed form and it was in fact for next weekend. What the hell?

"Oh God," I groaned as I looked at the signature.

Who the hell put Bryan Clifford in charge of this?

Bryan was our resident fuckup. He'd only gotten through the last three years of medical school because his mother was on the board and kept bailing him out. I prayed for anyone who had him as a doctor after we finished all of this. Lord, save me from mediocre white men.

I had no idea how it had gone from my name on Cézanne's list to Bryan ordering the wine and putting the wrong date on it.

"You're right. It is for next weekend."

"I'm really sorry," Sophia said.

"Do you have the wine in stock?"

"Sure, I have it, but my drivers are already gone for the day. I don't even have a van here tonight to deliver it myself."

My heart sank. "Can't you call someone?" I asked, teetering toward desperate. "It's, like, a three-thousand-dollar order. You'll lose that if we don't figure this out."

She shot me a pained expression. "I don't know who I could get to come in time. I can text a few drivers, but I'm sorry. It seems like a stretch, and I have a meeting after I close."

"I'd appreciate it. It would be really helpful. I don't know what else we're going to do."

Sophia patted my hand across the desk. "Let me shoot off those texts. Hopefully we can fix this."

"Thanks," I said with a sigh and then pulled out my phone to text Cézanne about the disaster. I had a feeling Bryan was about to get eaten alive by her after she found out.

I waited for news from Sophia when the bell over the door jingled.

I glanced up from my phone, praying to whoever would listen that one of the drivers had come back for some reason or another. Some serendipitous reason that would save my shitty day. We could pack up the van and drive out to the ranch, and I'd look like a hero.

Instead, I turned around and found the last person in Lubbock I wanted to see. The one person who had fractured my trust and left me a little more cynical than I'd been before. A line had been drawn in the sand. No matter that we'd had a one-night stand with the best sex of my life, I wouldn't open myself back up to be shattered by Jordan Wright again.

ABOUT THE AUTHOR

 K.A. Linde is the *USA Today* bestselling author of more than thirty novels. She has a Masters degree in political science from the University of Georgia, was the head campaign worker for the 2012 presidential campaign at the University of North Carolina at Chapel Hill, and served as the head coach of the Duke University dance team.

She loves reading fantasy novels, binge-watching Supernatural, traveling to far off destinations, baking insane desserts, and dancing in her spare time. She currently lives in Lubbock, Texas, with her husband and two super-adorable puppies.

Visit her online: www.kalinde.com
Facebook, Instagram, & Tiktok: @authorkalinde
For exclusive content www.kalinde.com/subscribe